OWL LAKE

by Tejima

Philomel Books

New York

Nestled deep in the mountains there lies a lake

that shimmers in the evening sun.

As the sun slips away, the sky darkens from gold to blue,

and a gentle stillness settles upon the land.

It is then that the owls come out.

Hungry after a day of sleep,

they start to search for breakfast.

Father Owl flies across the still, black water.

He keeps his
owl eyes open for
signs of silver fish.
But the lake is silent.

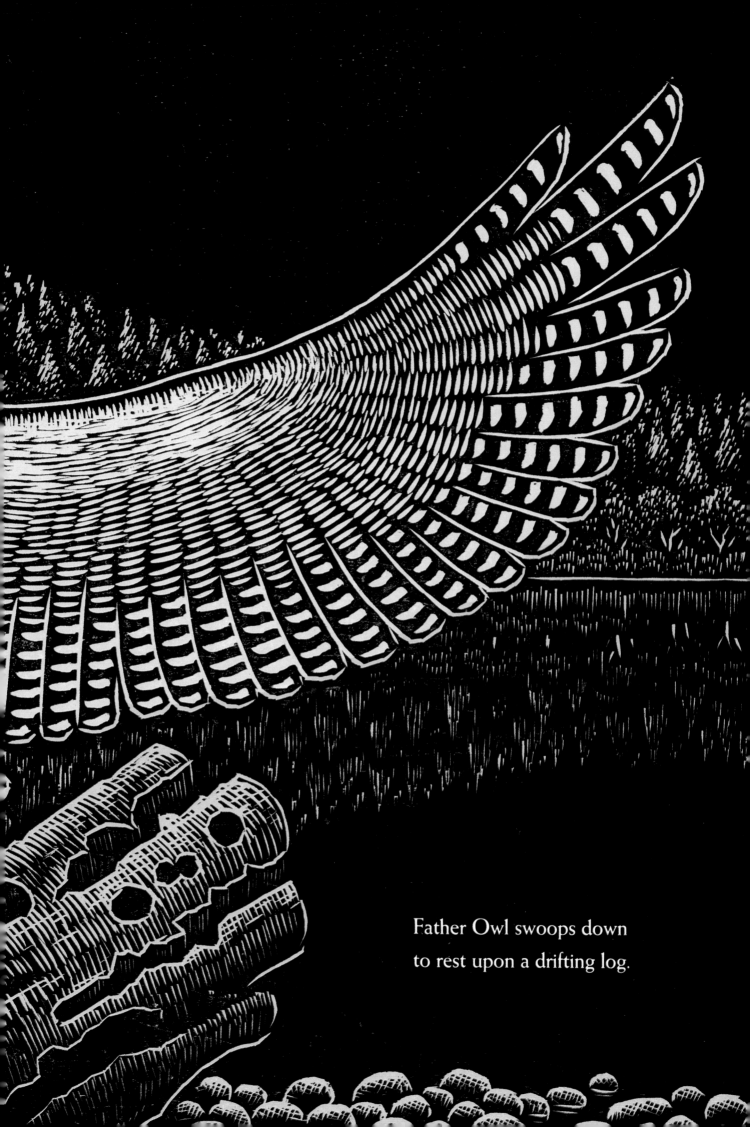

Father Owl swoops down
to rest upon a drifting log.

He closes his eyes in the darkness,

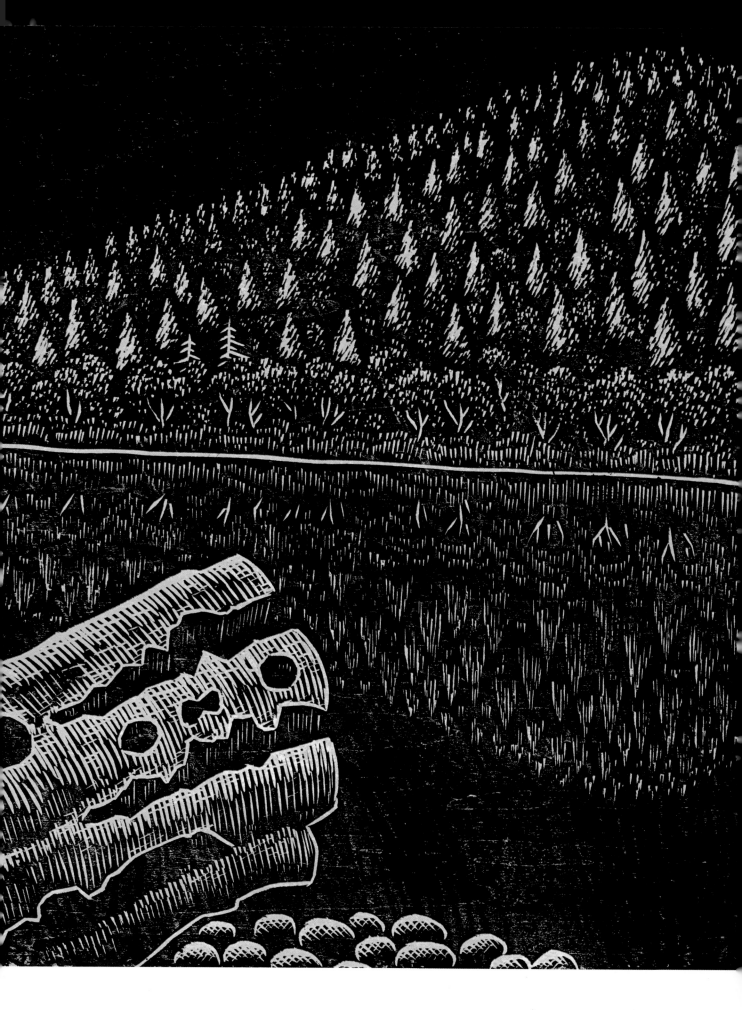

but even as he rests, he listens.

In the distance he hears the
WHOO WHOO WHOO
of his hungry owl family.

Suddenly from somewhere far away comes the sound of a fish jumping,

and the moon's reflection ripples across the lake.

Father Owl flaps
his mighty wings.
His feathers glisten
in the moonlit sky.

SWOOSH go his wings.

SWOOSH SWOOSH...

...faster and faster until

he sees the fish swimming right beneath him.

Clutching the silver fish, he rises from the lake,
his big wings spread across the night sky.

WHOO WHOO, he calls to his family.
WHOO WHOO, they answer.

Father Owl flies home.

The Owl Family eats breakfast under the glowing moon.

Next, it will be Mother Owl's turn to hunt.

Nestled deep in the mountains there lies a lake

that shimmers in the morning starlight.

As the stars fade away, the sky brightens from black
to blue and a gentle awakening settles upon the land.

It is then that the owls go to sleep.

Text and illustrations copyright © 1982 Keizaburo Tejima.
American text copyright © 1987 by Philomel Books. All rights
reserved. Published in the United States by Philomel Books, a
division of The Putnam Publishing Group, 51 Madison Avenue, New
York, NY 10010. Printed in Hong Kong by South China Printing Co.
Originally published by Fukutake Pub., Co., Ltd., Tokyo, Japan.

Library of Congress Cataloging-in-Publication Data Tejima,
Keizaburō. Owl lake. Translation of: Shimafurō no mizuumi
Summary: As the sun slips down behind the lake and the sky
darkens, Father Owl comes out and hunts for fish to feed his
hungry family. [1. Night — Fiction. 2. Owls — Fiction] I. Title.
PZ7.T234Ow 1987 [E] 86-25173 ISBN 0-399-21426-7
First impression